R0084245752

07/2016

D1515880

Here's what kids have to say about reading Magic Tree House® books and Magic Tree House® Merlin Missions:

Thank you for writing these great books! I have learned a great deal of information about history and the world around me.—Rosanna

Your series, the Magic Tree House, was really influential on my late childhood years. [Jack and Annie] taught me courage through their rigorous adventures and profound friendship, and how they stuck it out through thick and thin, from start to finish.—Joe

Your description is fantastic! The words pop out . . . oh, man . . . [the Magic Tree House series] is really exciting!—Christina

I like the Magic Tree House series. I stay up all night reading them. Even on school nights!—Peter

I think I've read about twenty-five of your Magic Tree House books! I'm reading every Magic Tree House book I can get my hands on!—Jack

Never stop writing, and if you can't think about anything to write about, don't worry, use some of my ideas!!—Kevin

Parents, teachers, and librarians love Magic Tree House® books, too!

[Magic Tree House] comes up quite a bit at parent/ teacher conferences. . . . The parents are amazed at how much more reading is being done at home because of your books. I am very pleased to know such fun and interesting reading exists for students. . . . Your books have also made students want to learn more about the places Jack and Annie visit. What wonderful starters for some research projects!—Kris L.

As a librarian, I have seen many happy young readers coming into the library to check out the next Magic Tree House book in the series. I have assisted young library patrons with finding nonfiction materials related to the Magic Tree House book they have read. . . . The message you are sending to children is invaluable: siblings can be friends; boys and girls can hang out together. . . .—Lynne H.

[My daughter] had a slow start reading, but somehow with your Magic Tree House series, she has been inspired and motivated to read. It is with such urgency that she tracks down your books. She often blurts out various facts and lines followed by "I read that in my Magic Tree House book."—Jenny E.

[My students] seize every opportunity they can to reread a Magic Tree House book or look at all the wonderful illustrations. Jack and Annie have opened a door to a world of literacy that I know will continue throughout the lives of my students. —Deborah H.

[My son] carries his Magic Tree House books everywhere he goes. He just can't put the book he is reading down until he finishes it. . . . He is doing better in school overall since he has made reading a daily thing. He even has a bet going with his aunt that if he continues doing well in school, she will continue to buy him the next book in the Magic Tree House series. —Rosalie R.

MAGIC TREE HOUSE® #33
A MERLIN MISSION

Carnival at Candlelight

by Mary Pope Osborne

illustrated by Sal Murdocca

A STEPPING STONE BOOK™

Random House 🏠 New York

Text copyright © 2005 by Mary Pope Osborne
Illustrations copyright © 2005 by Sal Murdocca

All rights reserved.
Published in the United States by Random House Children's Books, a division of Random House, Inc., New York. Originally published in hardcover by Random House Children's Books, a division of Random House, Inc., in 2005.

RANDOM HOUSE and colophon are registered trademarks and A STEPPING STONE BOOK and colophon are trademarks of Random House, Inc. MAGIC TREE HOUSE is a registered trademark of Mary Pope Osborne; used under license.

www.randomhouse.com/kids
www.magictreehouse.com

Educators and librarians, for a variety of teaching tools, visit us at
www.randomhouse.com/teachers

Library of Congress Cataloging-in-Publication Data
Osborne, Mary Pope.
Carnival at candlelight / by Mary Pope Osborne ; illustrated by Sal Murdocca.
    p. cm. — (Magic tree house ; #33)
SUMMARY: While on a mission to prove to Merlin that they can use magic wisely, Jack and Annie travel to eighteenth-century Venice, Italy, to save the city from disaster.
ISBN: 978-0-375-83033-4 (trade) — ISBN: 978-0-375-93033-1 (lib. bdg.) —
ISBN: 978-0-375-83034-1 (pbk.)
[1. Time travel—Fiction. 2. Magic—Fiction. 3. Tree houses—Fiction.
4. Brothers and sisters—Fiction. 5. Venice (Italy)—Fiction.]
I. Murdocca, Sal, ill. II. Title. III. Series: Osborne, Mary Pope.
Magic tree house series ; v #33.
PZ7.O81167Car 2005 [Fic]—dc22 2004018256

Printed in the United States of America
30 29 28 27 26 25 24 23

For Gail Hochman, of course

Dear Reader,

<u>Carnival at Candlelight</u> is the fifth book in a group of Magic Tree House books called the "Merlin Missions." On their first four Merlin Missions, Jack and Annie traveled to mythical lands, where many magical things took place. I love writing books that take place in fantasy worlds, but I also love writing books about real life. So the next Merlin Missions will combine the two—Jack and Annie will have fantasy adventures in real places in real times.

One of the most amazing places I've ever been

is the city of Venice, Italy. Venice is a group of islands in a lagoon between the Italian mainland and the Adriatic Sea. The water, the art, the architecture, the atmosphere—all make Venice one of the most beautiful cities in the world. Writing a Magic Tree House adventure set in Venice meant that I could return there in my imagination every day for many months. Working on this book was a very exciting journey. I invite you now to share my journey and discover the mystery and magic of Venice for yourself.

CONTENTS

I stood in Venice, on the Bridge of Sighs;
A palace and a prison on each hand:
I saw from out the wave her structures rise
As from the stroke of the enchanter's wand . . .
    —Lord Byron, *Childe Harold's Pilgrimage*

CHAPTER ONE

A Book of Magic

Dawn was breaking in the Frog Creek woods. Jack saw a light shining up ahead. He ran toward it. He ran so fast, he couldn't hear his feet hitting the ground. He couldn't feel the frosty winter air.

As Jack got closer to the light, he could see the magic tree house at the top of the tallest oak. A girl and boy were looking out the window. The girl had dark, wavy hair and sea-blue eyes. The boy had tousled red hair and a big grin on his face. As the two kids waved at him, Jack felt incredibly happy.

"Jack, wake up!"

Jack opened his eyes. His sister, Annie, was standing beside his bed. She was wearing her winter jacket. It was barely light outside.

"I just had a dream about the tree house," she said.

"Really?" Jack said sleepily.

"I dreamed we were running through the woods at dawn," said Annie, "and when we got to the tree house, Teddy and Kathleen were there waiting for us."

Jack sat up. "I just had the same dream!" he said.

"Meet you downstairs," said Annie.

Annie left Jack's room. Jack jumped out of bed, put on his glasses, and threw on his clothes. He grabbed his winter jacket and his backpack. Then he slipped quietly down the stairs and out the front door.

Annie was waiting on the porch. The February air was chilly. Frost sparkled in the grass as the sun rose over the Frog Creek woods.

"Ready?" asked Annie.

Jack nodded and zipped his jacket. Without another word, he and Annie hurried up their street and headed into the woods. They ran through the long shadows of early morning, between the bare winter trees. Then they stopped.

The tree house *was* back, just as Jack had seen it in his dream! It was high in the tallest oak tree, shining in the cold morning light.

"Wow," breathed Jack. "Dreams *can* come true."

"Yep," said Annie. "Teddy! Kathleen!"

No one answered.

"I guess only part of this dream came true," Annie said sadly. She grabbed the rope ladder and started up. Jack followed. Annie climbed into the tree house. "Oh, wow!" she said.

"What is it?" said Jack.

"They're here!" said Annie in a loud whisper.

Jack climbed in behind her. Their friends

Teddy and Kathleen, apprentices to Morgan le Fay, were sitting under the tree house window. Wrapped in heavy woolen cloaks, they were both fast asleep.

"Hey, sleepyheads!" said Annie. "Wake up!"

Kathleen blinked and yawned. Teddy rubbed his eyes. When he saw Jack and Annie, he gave them a wide grin and leapt to his feet. "Hello!" he said.

"Hello!" cried Annie. She threw her arms around Teddy. "We both dreamed you were here."

"Ah, then our magic worked!" said Teddy. "Kathleen suggested we send dreams to let you know we were here, and it seems our magic sent *us* to dreamland as well."

"But now we are all awake," said Kathleen. "And I am very glad to see you." She stood up, drawing her cloak around her. Her blue eyes sparkled like seawater in the dawn light.

"I'm glad to see you, too," Jack said shyly.

"Are you taking us on another Merlin Mission?" said Annie.

"Not exactly," said Teddy. "Merlin has a most important mission for you. But this time, we will not be going along."

"Oh, no!" said Annie. "What if we need your magic to help us?"

Teddy and Kathleen looked at each other and smiled. Then Kathleen turned back to Jack and Annie. "Morgan thinks you may be ready to use magic on your own," she said.

"Really?" said Jack.

"Yes," said Teddy, "but Merlin is *very* cautious about sharing magic powers with mortals, even with two as worthy as you. He is also wary of magic being used outside the realm of Camelot. Nevertheless, Morgan has convinced Merlin to let you prove yourselves. You will be tested on four missions."

"But we don't know any magic," said Jack.

"Remember what I told you on our last

adventure?" said Teddy. "If we all work together—"

"Anything is possible!" said Annie. "But you just said you weren't coming with us."

"That is true," said Kathleen. "And that is why we bring you *this*." She reached into a pocket of her cloak and pulled out a small hand-made book. She gave the book to Annie.

The cover of the book was made of rough brown paper. Written on it in neat, simple handwriting was the title:

10
Magic Rhymes
for
Annie and Jack
from
Teddy and Kathleen

"You made this for us?" said Annie.

"Yes," said Kathleen. "One line of each rhyme is in Teddy's language, and one is in mine, the language of the Seal People."

Annie opened the book to the table of contents. She and Jack skimmed the list of rhymes, and Jack read some of the entries aloud:

"*Fly Through the Air. Make Metal Soft. Turn into Ducks—*"

Annie giggled. "These are so cool!" she said. "Let's all turn into ducks!"

"Not now," said Kathleen. "You must use these rhymes very sparingly. There are only ten rhymes in the book, and each can only be used once. They are meant to last you for four journeys."

"Four?" said Jack.

"Aye," said Teddy. "Merlin has agreed that if you can use our magic wisely on four missions, he will teach you the secrets that will allow you to make magic on your own."

"Oh, boy!" said Annie.

Jack put the book of magic rhymes in his backpack. "So where are we going on our first mission?" he asked.

"This research book from Morgan will tell you," said Teddy. He took out a book and handed it to Jack. The cover showed a bright, colorful city surrounded by water.

Jack read the title aloud:

A VISIT TO VENICE, ITALY.

"I've heard of Venice," said Annie. "Last year Aunt Gail and Uncle Michael went there on vacation."

"Aye, 'tis a city that has long welcomed travelers," said Teddy. "But you and Jack will travel to the Venice of two hundred sixty years ago."

"What will we do there?" asked Jack.

"Merlin has prepared careful directions for you," said Teddy. He pulled a letter out of a pocket in his cloak and gave it to Jack. "Read this when you get to Venice."

"Okay," said Jack. He put Merlin's letter and Morgan's research book into his backpack.

"Wait a minute," said Annie. "If we take the tree house to Venice, how will you guys get back to Camelot?"

Teddy and Kathleen smiled and held up their hands. They each wore a ring made of pale blue glass. "These magic rings belong to Morgan," said Kathleen. "They will take us home."

"Remember," Teddy said to Jack and Annie. "Follow Merlin's directions carefully. If you prove yourselves to be wise and brave helpers, he will call for you again soon."

Kathleen nodded. "Good-bye now," she said to Jack and Annie. "Good luck."

Kathleen and Teddy raised their glass rings to their lips. Together they whispered words too softly to be heard, then blew on the rings.

Before Jack and Annie's eyes, the two young sorcerers began to fade into the cool morning air. In an instant, they had disappeared completely.

"They're gone," breathed Jack.

"I guess it's time for us to go, too," said Annie.

Jack took a deep breath. Then he pointed at the cover of the Venice book. "I wish we could go there!" he said.

The wind started to blow.

The tree house started to spin.

It spun faster and faster.

Then everything was still.

Absolutely still.

CHAPTER TWO

Carnival

Annie laughed.

Jack opened his eyes. He and Annie were wearing purple and pink outfits with huge ruffled collars. On their heads were funny hats. On their feet were red slippers with big bows.

"Who are we?" Annie asked.

"I don't know," said Jack. He didn't feel like a wise and brave helper in his red slippers. He felt stupid.

Together Jack and Annie looked out the tree house window. They had landed in a small tree inside a walled garden. The sky was gray. Jack couldn't tell if it was morning or evening, but the air felt damp and heavy, as if a storm was about to break.

"I guess this is Venice," he said.

"Let's check our book," said Annie. She opened their research book and read aloud:

> Today the city of Venice (say VEN-iss) is one of the most popular tourist spots in the world. It lies in a lagoon of the Adriatic Sea. Instead of roads, Venice has waterways called canals. People glide along the canals in shallow boats called gondolas (GON-duh-luz). A man called a gondolier (gon-duh-LEER) stands in the back of the boat and uses a long oar to propel the gondola through the water.

"That sounds like fun," said Jack.

"Yep," said Annie. She closed the book. "Let's go."

"Wait," said Jack. "We don't even know what our mission is yet." He took out Merlin's letter and unfolded it. He read aloud:

Dear Jack and Annie of Frog Creek,
Your mission will require great patience and a bit of magic. The Grand Lady of the Lagoon is in terrible danger. The only one who can help you save her from disaster is the Ruler of the Seas. To locate him, follow these directions:

When waters rise beneath the moon,
Visit the Grand Lady of the Lagoon.
To find out where you need to go,
Seek out a painter named Tiepolo.
At midnight two men will tell you the time.
To the top of their tower hurry and climb.
The King of the Jungle will carry you there,
Not over land, but high in the air.
An angel of gold will show you the way
To the sea by night, and home by day.
                                        —M.

Jack pushed his glasses into place. "Hmm," he said.

"I wonder who the Grand Lady is," said Annie. "And why do we need to save her?"

"I'm wondering lots of stuff," said Jack. "What about the King of the Jungle? We're in a city, not a jungle. And what about that angel? And—"

"Let's just take one thing at a time," said Annie. "What are we supposed to do first?"

Jack looked back at the letter and read:

When waters rise beneath the moon,
Visit the Grand Lady of the Lagoon.

"So let's start by finding the Grand Lady," said Annie. She headed down the tree house ladder.

Jack put Merlin's letter into his backpack, along with Morgan's research book and Teddy and Kathleen's book of magic rhymes. Then he climbed down the rope ladder and caught up with Annie.

Jack and Annie walked over a pebbly path as the sky darkened. *Good*, thought Jack. *It's night.*

He didn't want anyone to see him in his silly outfit—especially the red slippers with the bows.

"That must be the way out," said Annie. She led Jack to a wooden gate in the garden wall and pushed it open.

Jack and Annie stepped through the gate onto a quiet, empty walkway. Next to the walkway was a narrow lane of water.

"I guess that's a canal," said Jack.

"And that must be a gondola," said Annie. She pointed to a long, curved black boat rounding the corner. In the last light of day, the gondola was gliding silently up the canal toward them.

"Yikes," whispered Annie.

There were two people in the boat—a gondolier and a passenger. Each wore a black cloak, white gloves, and a ghostly white mask. The masks had long, pointy noses shaped like bird beaks. The passenger sat in the middle of the boat, holding a lantern. The gondolier stood in the back, pushing a long oar through the water.

"They look a lot weirder than us," said Annie.

"No kidding," said Jack.

"Hello!" the passenger shouted.

The person's voice was muffled behind the white mask. "Do you need help?"

"Yes!" Annie shouted back. "Can you take us to the Grand Lady of the Lagoon?"

"Yes, of course. She is back that way!" answered the masked passenger. "Come."

"Great!" said Annie. She grabbed Jack's hand and pulled him over to the gondola. The gondola rocked a bit as she and Jack climbed aboard and took seats between the gondolier and the passenger.

The gondolier pushed the gondola away from the landing. His long oar made soft splashes in the water as the boat moved up the canal.

Jack cleared his throat. "Um, excuse me," he said. "Why are you wearing bird masks?"

"For Carnival, of course," said the passenger. "That is why you are wearing clown costumes, no?"

"Oh, yeah, sure," said Jack.

As the gondola slid through the canal, Jack snuck their research book out of his backpack.

"Oh, boy, a carnival!" Annie whispered to Jack. "I hope it has a roller coaster."

"I don't think they had roller coasters two hundred sixty years ago," whispered Jack.

Jack looked up *carnival* in the index. He

found the page. Then he and Annie silently read together:

> **For many centuries, Carnival has been the most famous yearly festival of Venice. For Carnival, people disguise themselves as anything they want to be. Rich, poor, male, female, young, and old—all are equal during Carnival.**

"Look, that's us," whispered Annie. She pointed to a picture of a colorful costume with a white ruffled collar and red slippers with bows.

"Yeah, and that's them," whispered Jack. He pointed to a picture of a person dressed in a black cloak and a white mask with a bird's beak.

Jack closed the book and put it away. The gondola people didn't seem so weird anymore. But he still wondered why a grand lady was in terrible danger at Carnival.

As the boat glided around a bend, Jack caught his breath. He saw dozens of gondolas rocking on the choppy waters of a wide, open canal. They were all decorated with ribbons and flowers. Candlelight from their lanterns danced on the dark, rippling water.

"Look, that must be Carnival over there," said Annie, pointing.

In the distance, thousands of candles twinkled along the shoreline. Sounds of laughter, clapping, and shouting floated over the water.

"Hold on tightly!" said the masked person in the front of the gondola. "The tide is high tonight!" As their gondola joined the fleet of boats heading toward Carnival, the wind picked up. The waves grew taller.

Jack and Annie held on to the sides of the boat. Jack heard a faint rumble of faraway thunder. He saw a zigzag flash of lightning in the distant sky. *Is a storm coming?* he wondered nervously. *Is the storm part of the disaster that's going to happen to the Grand Lady of the Lagoon?*

"This is going to be fun, isn't it?" said Annie cheerfully.

"Sure," said Jack. He tried to shake off his worries as the wind and tide helped push the gondola toward the twinkling candles of Carnival.

CHAPTER THREE

The Grand Lady of the Lagoon

The gondola glided toward a landing at the edge of the canal. As the gondolier tied up the boat, water was sloshing from the canal onto a wide walkway filled with Carnival-goers.

The gondolier reached a gloved hand toward Annie and helped her out of the boat. He then held out a hand to Jack. When Jack grabbed it, he was surprised that the gondolier's hand felt small under the white glove, like a kid's hand.

As soon as Jack had stepped out of the boat, the gondolier untied the rope, pushed off from the landing, and began rowing away.

"Bye! Thanks!" called Annie.

The two strangers in the white bird masks waved.

Jack and Annie watched the gondola disappear over the choppy waters. Then they looked back at the shore. The Carnival crowd was parading up and down the wide walkway along the canal.

"Hey, look," said Annie. "There's a bunch of people dressed like us! And like the two people in our gondola!"

Jack saw lots of black cloaks, bird masks, funny hats, and ruffled collars. He also saw people dressed as chickens, pirates, and knights. None of the costumed people seemed to mind the water spilling over the edge of the canal, soaking their boots and slippers.

As Jack and Annie stared at the crowd, a distant bell began to ring. The bell rang nine times. "I guess that means it's nine o'clock," said Jack.

Just then another bell began to chime. Jack counted again. This time, *ten* chimes rang out. "Ten?" said Jack, puzzled. "So what time is it? Nine o'clock or ten o'clock?"

"Don't worry about that now," said Annie. "I think I see the Grand Lady of the Lagoon!"

"Where?" said Jack.

Annie pointed to a tall woman at the edge of the parade. She was wearing a black mask. She wore piles of jewelry, a white wig, and a wide hoop skirt.

Jack and Annie moved toward the lady. "Excuse me," said Annie. "Hi."

The lady looked at Annie. "Hello," she said in a deep man's voice.

"Whoa," said Jack, stepping back.

Annie laughed. "You're a man!" she said.

"Of course," said the man. "But for Carnival, I am a very beautiful lady, no?"

"We're looking for someone called the Grand Lady of—" started Annie. But before she could finish, a giant chicken grabbed the man's hand and pulled him away into the crowd.

"Oh, brother," said Jack, looking around. Lots of people were dressed as grand ladies! "How are we supposed to know who to visit?"

"Maybe it's time to use one of Kathleen and Teddy's rhymes," said Annie.

"No, we should save our rhymes," said Jack.

"Then let's just skip visiting the Grand Lady of the Lagoon for now," said Annie. "What's the *next* thing Merlin tells us to do?"

Jack looked at Merlin's directions and read aloud:

To find out where you need to go,
Seek out a painter named Tiepolo.

"Good, that's clear," said Jack. "Let's see if Tiepolo is in our research book."

As the noisy crowd celebrated around them, Jack pulled out the book. He stood near a lantern and looked in the index. "He's here!" said Jack. He turned to the right page and read:

Tiepolo (say tee-EP-uh-lo) was one of the greatest painters of Venice in the 1700s. He painted bright, beautiful oil paintings for palaces and villas.

"If the guy's so famous, people must know where he lives," said Annie. "Excuse me!" she called to a clown walking by. "Can you tell us where the painter Tiepolo lives?"

"Near the Church of San Felice," the clown said.

"Thanks!" said Annie.

"But you won't find him home now," the clown called over his shoulder. "He's in Milan, painting."

"Where's that?" shouted Jack.

"Over a day's ride on horseback," said the clown. Then he disappeared into the crowd.

"Hmmm . . . ," said Annie. "Do you think Merlin wants us to go to Milan?"

"We don't have time," said Jack. "I think we have to skip Tiepolo, too."

"Yeah," said Annie. "Hey, maybe we should just skip all this stuff and try to find the Ruler of the Seas on our own. Our letter says he's the only one who can help us save the Grand Lady."

"I don't know . . . ," said Jack. "In his letter, Merlin tells us to be patient—"

But Annie was already calling to a pirate passing by. "Sir, do you know where we can find the Ruler of the Seas?"

"What?" shouted the pirate.

"The ruler! Do you know where he lives?" yelled Annie.

"In the palace on Saint Mark's Square!" said the pirate.

"Where's that?" Annie called. But the pirate had disappeared into the crowd.

"I'll look up Saint Mark's Square," said Jack. He turned the pages of their book until he came to a map of Venice. "Oh, cool," he said. Jack loved maps.

"Okay, let's see," Jack said. "We're *here*." He

pointed to the walkway along the canal on the map. "And we want to go to Saint Mark's Square." He pointed to another place on the map. "It's really close."

"Yeah, and it looks like everyone else is headed there, too," said Annie. "Come on."

"So, if we go this way . . . ," said Jack. He traced their route with his finger.

"Come on, Jack!" called Annie.

Jack looked up from the map. Annie was already walking with the crowd. Jack closed the book and hurried after her. Soon they came to a huge, open square.

"Wow," Jack said breathlessly. Saint Mark's Square was filled with candlelight and musicians. Acrobats balanced on tightropes. Boxers boxed in a ring. Knights fenced with swords. Clowns walked on tall stilts, raced wheelbarrows, and tried to catch live eels in their mouths. All around the square were candlelit buildings.

"Venice is beautiful," said Annie.

"Yeah," said Jack. He looked back at their book.

He found an illustration of Saint Mark's Square. Jack read the descriptions of the buildings:

> **The watchtower of Saint Mark's Square is the tallest building in Venice. The weather vane on top once helped sailors by showing them which way the wind was blowing.**

Jack looked up. "I can barely see the weather vane up there," he said. "But I think it's pointing north. So the wind must be blowing from the south."

"What about the ruler's palace? Where's that?" asked Annie.

Jack read on:

> **The clock tower is one of the most beautiful towers in the world. On top of the tower, a bell is struck every hour by—**

"Jack, skip to the ruler's palace!" interrupted Annie. "Please!"

"Okay, okay," said Jack. He read about the palace:

The palace of Venice's ruler is one of the most splendid structures ever built. It has a great hall where as many as 2,000 nobles once met to discuss city matters. It also holds the city's grim prison cells. Above the palace door is a sculpture of Saint Mark showing a book to a winged lion—

"There's the palace door!" said Annie.

Jack looked up from the map. Annie was heading toward a huge door with the sculpture of a man and a winged lion above it. Jack closed the book and hurried to catch up to her.

A guard was standing by the palace door. The guard wore a uniform and held a rifle. "Wait," Jack whispered. "Is he a real guard? Or is that just a costume?"

"I'll find out," said Annie. She walked over to the guard. "Excuse me, sir. Is the ruler of Venice inside the palace now?"

"Begone, clown!" the guard said gruffly.

"But it's important," said Annie. "We need to talk to him about something."

"I said begone!" the guard growled. "I am tired of clowns wasting my time!"

"She's not really a clown," said Jack, coming forward. "We're on a mission. We—"

"Go! Both of you! Or else!" roared the guard. He held up his rifle. *He's definitely not wearing a costume*, thought Jack.

"Okay, sorry, sorry," said Jack. He and Annie moved away from the palace entrance.

"What a grouchy guy," said Annie.

"He'll never let us in," said Jack.

"Maybe it's time to use one of Teddy and Kathleen's rhymes," said Annie. "Maybe we should turn into ducks. The guard wouldn't mind if a couple of ducks—"

"No," said Jack. "We have to save our rhymes."

"Well, how will we get inside?" Annie asked.

"Patience," said Jack. "Remember—"

Before he could finish, Annie broke in, "Hey, look!"

Two clowns on stilts were dancing around the guard. One grabbed the guard's rifle and tossed it to the other.

"Hey!" the guard yelled. "Give that back!"

"Now's our chance!" said Annie. "Quick!" She ran to the entrance and slipped through the door.

"Oh, no—oh, man!" said Jack. While the guard chased after the two clowns on stilts, Jack rushed to the doorway of the palace and slipped inside, too.

CHAPTER FOUR

Rats!

Jack found Annie standing behind a column in a lantern-lit courtyard. The courtyard was quiet and empty. "Everyone in Venice must be at Carnival," said Jack. "I just hope the ruler is home."

"Yeah, we'll ask him if he knows the Grand Lady of the Lagoon," said Annie. "And we'll tell him he has to help us save her from a terrible disaster."

Jack looked at his map of the palace. Several rooms were labeled *Ruler's Living Chambers*. "I

guess that's where he lives," said Jack. "We have to go up some stairs called the Giants' Stairs to get there."

"The Giants' Stairs?" said Annie.

"Yeah," said Jack. "Listen to this."

These stairs are called the Giants' Stairs because they are guarded by two large statues of gods from Roman mythology: Mars, the god of war, and Neptune, the god of the sea.

"Cool," said Annie. "Let's go."

Jack and Annie hurried down the passageway that ran along the courtyard until they came to a wide staircase. On either side of the stairs were giant marble statues of strong-looking men.

"Mars and Neptune," said Jack. "This is it. Come on."

Jack and Annie quickly climbed the Giants' Stairs. At the top, Jack looked at the map again. "Now we turn right and head for the Golden Staircase," he said.

Keeping an eye out for more guards, they crept down a hall until they came to a fancy staircase under a gold ceiling.

"There it is," said Jack. "Let's climb up." He and Annie hurried up the Golden Staircase. When they got to the top, they froze. Another guard was slouched against the wall by the stairs. His eyes were closed, and he was snoring softly.

Jack motioned to Annie, and they tiptoed past the sleeping guard to the entrance of the ruler's living chambers. Jack glanced at the map. "This is it," he whispered.

The door was open. Jack and Annie peeked inside. "Knock, knock?" Annie said in a soft voice.

No one answered.

They stepped through the doorway. A fire blazed on the hearth. Overhead many candles burned brightly. The dancing flames cast shadows on a marble floor and a carved gold ceiling.

"I have a feeling the ruler's not here," said Annie. "Maybe we should leave."

Jack looked at their book. "Wait, the next room is the Map Room," he said. "Let's just take a look."

"Okay, but we'd better hurry," said Annie.

Jack led the way into the Map Room. Colorful maps hung on the walls. In the middle of the floor were two huge globes. Jack sighed. "I *love* this room," he said.

"Look, more lions," said Annie. She pointed to three paintings of winged lions on one of the walls. "Why are there lions with wings everywhere?"

Jack looked up *winged lions* in their book. He turned to the right page and read:

The winged lion is the symbol of Venice. Represented in paintings and sculptures all over the city, the lions stand for strength on both land and sea.

As Jack and Annie looked back up at the lion paintings, they heard footsteps. The grouchy guard and the sleepy guard rushed into the room.

"Hi, we're looking—" began Annie.

"There they are! The thieves!" the sleepy guard shouted at the grouchy guard. "I *told* you I heard voices!"

"We're not thieves," said Annie. "We were just looking for your ruler to ask for his help."

"She's right," said Jack. "We have to tell him that—"

"Won't admit your crime, eh?" said the grouchy guard. "The worst cells are reserved for criminals like you! Move!"

"But we—" started Annie.

"Move!" shouted the grouchy guard, raising his rifle and pointing to the door.

Jack knew there was no use arguing. He took Annie's hand and led her out of the ruler's living chambers. The two guards walked behind them, pointing guns at their backs.

"To the end of the hall and down the steps!" growled the grouchy guard.

Jack and Annie walked quickly down the hall, then down some steep, narrow steps. They moved through a low stone corridor, the guards close behind them.

"Over the Bridge of Sighs!" shouted the grouchy guard. "And be sure to sigh when you cross it—because you won't be coming back for a long time!"

Jack gripped Annie's hand as they crossed a covered footbridge to another building. Once inside, they started down a lantern-lit hallway filled with puddles. Jack's shoes felt squishy and soggy as he sloshed through the water.

"Halt!" shouted the grouchy guard.

Jack and Annie stopped in front of a heavy wooden door. The grouchy guard opened the door and pushed them into a dark, damp cell.

The door slammed shut. Jack heard a heavy metal bolt clank into place. Then he heard the guards splash away down the hall, arguing with each other.

The prison was eerily quiet. It was hard to breathe in the stale cell. It was hard to see, too. Only the dim light of the hallway shone faintly through the barred window. Under the window was a wooden bench.

"What now?" Annie asked in a small voice.

For a moment, Jack couldn't answer. He was stunned. Minutes ago they'd been at the bright Carnival. Now they were locked in a dingy prison cell. "I—I'll look in the book," he said.

Jack felt shaky as he opened their research book. He moved close to the barred window to read by the dim light. He looked up *prison* in the index. He found it and read aloud:

> **The prison cells at ground level in the palace were called the pozzi, meaning "wells" or "pits." They were dank, airless, and filled with rats. Even the government eventually decided they were too cruel.**

Jack heard a squeak from a dark corner. He stopped reading and looked up. He heard the squeak again. The hair went up on his neck. *Was that a rat?* he wondered.

"Was that a rat?" said Annie.

The squeak came again from the dark corner. Then a squeak came from another corner. Jack heard rustling along the walls and more squeaking.

"Oh, man," he breathed. *There were rats everywhere.*

"I think it's time for magic," said Annie.

"Yep," said Jack, "definitely." He kept his eye on the dark corners while Annie reached into his backpack and pulled out Teddy and Kathleen's book.

Annie read from the table of contents: *"Make a Stone Come Alive. Make Metal Soft. Turn into Ducks."* Annie looked up. "Are rats afraid of ducks?" she asked.

"Forget ducks!" said Jack. "Go back to *Make Metal Soft*—that's what we need to do! You read the rhyme, and I'll try to pull the bars apart."

"Okay, good," said Annie.

Jack jumped onto the wooden bench under the barred window. The squeaking grew louder.

Jack reached up and felt the iron bars. They were cold and hard and very solid. Jack couldn't imagine bending them.

The squeaks were getting louder. Jack gripped two bars in the middle of the window and took a deep breath. "Read the rhyme!" he said.

Annie read aloud:

Iron or copper, brass or steel,
Bree-on-saw! Bro-on-beel!

As Annie finished the rhyme, the bars began to glow. They grew warmer in Jack's hands. "I think it's working!" he cried.

Holding the bars tightly, Jack pulled in opposite directions. Slowly the glowing bars began to stretch and bend. Jack pulled till there was an opening large enough for Annie and him to fit through.

"We did it!" he cried.

"Great! Hurry, hurry! The rats are coming!" cried Annie as she jumped on the bench.

Jack heard a chorus of squeaks from all sides of the cell. He looked down. He saw the shadowy shapes of dozens of rats. They seemed to be sniffing the air below the window.

"Go! Go!" Jack cried to Annie.

Annie squeezed between the bars and jumped down into the hallway. Jack followed her. He hit the wet floor and scrambled to his feet. "Come on!" he cried.

Jack and Annie sloshed down the watery hallway. At the end of it, they nearly bumped right into the two guards. Jack and Annie kept running.

"Hey!" the grouchy guard shouted, running after them. He reached for Jack. The other guard tried to catch Annie.

Jack and Annie dodged away from them. The guards crashed into each other, falling to the floor. Jack and Annie kept running. They dashed across the Bridge of Sighs. They ran through the corridor and up the steep stone steps.

"This way!" cried Jack. He and Annie tore down the hall, heading for the Golden Staircase.

"Hey! Hey!" the guards yelled from far behind.

Jack and Annie bounded down the Golden Staircase two steps at a time. They flew down the hall and down the Giants' Stairs. They ran past the statues of Mars and Neptune and charged down the long, open passageway. Finally, they dashed through the entrance of the palace and escaped into Saint Mark's Square.

CHAPTER FIVE

Lorenzo

Jack and Annie ran through the square, dodging dancers, fortune-tellers, and acrobats. They didn't stop until they were hidden in the middle of a crowd watching a puppet show.

As Jack tried to catch his breath, he looked around at all the pirate and animal and clown costumes. He was glad now that he and Annie were dressed in silly outfits, too. When they looked at each other, they laughed nervously.

"Maybe we shouldn't have skipped ahead," said Jack.

"Yeah, you were right," said Annie. "We should have been more patient. Let's go back to the part about the painter Tiepolo."

Jack nodded. "I think we should go to his house," he said. "Maybe he's there after all. Maybe that clown had the wrong information."

"I hope so," said Annie.

"The clown said Tiepolo lives near the Church of San Felice," said Jack. He pulled out their map and studied it. "Okay, so we're here in Saint

Mark's Square. And we have to get *there*." He traced the route with his finger. "Got it. Let's go. Stay in the shadows in case those guards come looking for us."

Jack stuffed the book into his backpack. Annie grabbed his hand, and together they squeezed through the Carnival crowd until they came to an alley off the square.

The wind was blowing harder as Jack and Annie headed down one shadowy alley, then another. They walked between rows of tightly

packed shops, cafés, and houses. As they walked farther from Saint Mark's Square, the streets became less crowded.

After a while, they came to a small footbridge that crossed a canal. As they hurried over the bridge, Jack noticed water washing onto the sidewalks. "What's going on with the water?" he said.

"Let's ask *her*," said Annie. She pointed to a young woman locking up a café. The woman wore a blue mask and a lacy purple dress. Water was swirling around her high black shoes.

"Excuse me," said Annie, "do you know why there's so much water in the streets?"

"Oh, there has been much rain in the mountains," said the young woman. "It all washes down to the lagoon. It makes the water very high."

"Is that dangerous?" asked Jack.

The woman smiled. "Oh, no," she said. "We often have high water here in Venice. You shouldn't worry. You should go watch the fireworks on the waterfront near Saint Mark's. Everyone is going there."

"Thanks!" said Annie.

The woman waved and went on her way.

"I guess we can stop worrying about the water," Annie said to Jack.

"Yeah," said Jack. But he couldn't help worrying as he saw a clump of seaweed wash past them down the alley.

As Jack and Annie walked toward the Church of San Felice, a bell started to chime. Jack counted the bongs: *eleven.* Another bell started to toll. Jack counted *ten* bongs. "What time do you think it is, really?" he asked. "I don't understand."

"Patience, remember?" said Annie. "One thing at a time. We just have to find Tiepolo's house now."

Soon they came to the small Church of San Felice. The square next to the church was empty except for an old man walking a small, fat dog.

"Good evening, little clowns," the man said with a friendly smile. "Why aren't you at the waterfront by Saint Mark's Square? I'd be there myself, except my Rosa is afraid of fireworks." He smiled at his chubby dog.

"Actually, we're trying to find the house of a painter named Tiepolo," said Jack.

"Oh, he is my neighbor," said the old man. "He lives there—" He pointed to a dark house off the square. "But you won't find him home."

"I know, we heard he's away," said Jack. "We were just wondering if he was coming back soon."

"I fear not," said the man. "Tiepolo told everyone that he would be gone for many months. But you should get along to the fireworks on the waterfront now. Everyone in Venice will be there to see them. They are quite magnificent on the last night of Carnival."

"Thanks," said Jack.

The old man waved. As he and Rosa walked slowly across the square, the church bell began to sound. It bonged eleven times.

"Excuse me, sir," Jack called. "All the clocks in Venice tell different times. Which one is right?"

"None!" the old man called. "That is one of the wonderful things about our city. Venice is timeless!" The man laughed, and he and Rosa went inside a small yellow house.

Jack sat down on a bench in the square. He put his head in his hands. Annie sat next to him. "I guess we *do* have to skip Tiepolo," she said. "What's the next thing Merlin tells us to do?"

Jack sighed. He pulled out the magician's letter and read the next two lines:

At midnight two men will tell you the time.

To the top of their tower hurry and climb.

"Oh, great," said Jack. "How will we know if it's really midnight? The man just said none of the clocks are right because Venice is timeless."

"According to Merlin, two men will tell us the right time," said Annie. "Two men who own some kind of tower we have to climb."

"Right," said Jack. "But that makes no sense, either. Who are they? How are we supposed to find them? We'll have to skip that part, too. We're skipping our whole mission, whatever it is. A terrible disaster's about to happen to some Grand Lady of the Lagoon, and we have no idea who she is. We don't know what the disaster is. We don't know where to find the Ruler of the Seas or how to find a painter named Tiepolo—or even how to tell the right time! We're completely failing Merlin's test!"

"Calm down. We just have to be patient," said Annie. "Everything will make sense soon."

"*How* soon?" said Jack. He felt cold and wet and miserable.

"*Very* soon . . . ," said Annie. "In fact, I think I see a light now inside Tiepolo's house." She stood up. "I definitely see a light!"

Annie ran over to the small house off the square. She peeped through a window. "Jack!" she called in a loud whisper. "Come here!"

Jack walked over to her. "Someone's painting in there," said Annie.

Through the window, Jack saw a candle burning in a corner of the room. He saw canvases and pots of paint. He saw a boy standing at an easel. The boy was painting a picture on a large canvas.

"He's just a kid," said Jack with disappointment. "He can't be Tiepolo."

"So what?" said Annie. "Maybe he can help us." She tapped on the glass.

The boy looked up. He carried his candle to the window and opened it. He had reddish brown hair and big eyes. "Hello," he said. "Are you looking for someone?"

"I'm Annie, and this is my brother, Jack," said Annie. "We're visiting Venice. And we were hoping to find a painter named Tiepolo."

"You have just done so," the boy said. "My name is Lorenzo Tiepolo." Lorenzo had a very serious manner.

"You're a painter, too?" asked Annie.

"Yes. As you can see, I am painting right now. I help my father and my older brother with their paintings," said Lorenzo. "And when they are gone, I paint my own. I will even miss the last night of Carnival to paint. But why are you not there?"

"We're on a mission," said Annie. "We just escaped from the palace prison. We got caught looking for the Ruler of the Seas."

"The Ruler of the Seas?" said Lorenzo. "Why were you looking in the palace? The Ruler of the Seas is right here."

"What?" said Jack. "The Ruler of the Seas is *here*?"

Lorenzo smiled. Then he walked to a large covered canvas propped against the wall. He pulled off the cloth cover. He held up his candle to show a painting of a beautiful woman resting her hand on the head of a golden lion. A man was giving coins to the woman. The man had a bare chest, a rugged face, long dark hair, and a white beard. Behind him was a three-pronged fishing spear.

"My father has been working on this painting for some time," said Lorenzo. He pointed at the bearded man. "'Tis Neptune."

"Neptune?" said Jack. "He's one of the gods in Roman mythology, right?"

"Yes, the Ruler of the Seas," said Lorenzo.

"Ohhh . . . We thought the Ruler of the Seas

was the ruler of Venice," said Annie. "We thought he lived in the palace on Saint Mark's Square."

Lorenzo laughed. "Oh, no, the palace is just the home of our city's human ruler," he said. "The true ruler of all the seas is Neptune."

"Where does Neptune live, Lorenzo?" Annie asked.

"He lives beneath the water in a beautiful palace made of coral and sparkling jewels," said Lorenzo. "But only a few people can actually see Neptune."

"Like who?" asked Annie.

"Those with imaginations, like my father, my brother, and myself," said Lorenzo. "We have heard the waves around Neptune roar like wild bulls. We have seen his fishing spear rising high above the surface of the sea, gleaming in the moonlight."

"That sounds great," said Annie.

"Yeah, great," Jack said politely. "You guys must have really good imaginations. Thanks,

Lorenzo." He turned to Annie. "I'm going to look at the research book some more."

Jack walked back to the bench and pulled out their book. He felt totally discouraged. Neptune wasn't a real person. They'd come to *another* dead end.

Annie stayed by the window. "Lorenzo, one more question," she said. "Why is Neptune giving a gift to that lady?"

"Neptune is offering the riches of the sea to Venice," answered Lorenzo.

"So the lady in the painting is supposed to be the city of Venice?" said Annie.

"Yes," said Lorenzo. "This is how my father thinks of Venice. She is the Grand Lady of the Lagoon."

Jack looked up from the book. He felt goose bumps on his skin.

"Thanks, Lorenzo!" said Annie. "You helped us a lot!"

"You are welcome, Annie," said Lorenzo. "Good night." Then he closed the window.

"Jack! Jack!" said Annie, hurrying to him. "The Grand Lady of the Lagoon is Venice!"

"I know! I heard!" said Jack.

"Now I understand our mission," said Annie. "We have to save *Venice* from a terrible disaster. We have to save *all of Venice*!"

CHAPTER SIX

Disaster

"We have to save all of Venice?" said Jack. "That's a big responsibility. What do we have to save Venice *from*?"

"Well, if Neptune's going to help us, it must have something to do with water," said Annie.

"Yeah, like the water that's flooding the alleys," said Jack.

"But the woman at the café told us not to worry about that," said Annie.

"I'm still worried," said Jack. "Let's look up *floods* in our Venice book." He found *floods* in the index. He turned to the right page and read:

Most of the time, high water in Venice is not serious. But if several conditions are present at the same time, a flood disaster can occur.

"A flood disaster! That must be it!" said Annie. "So what are the conditions?"

"It lists them here," said Jack. He read:

A high tide
Strong winds from the south
Heavy flow of water from the mountains
Severe storms at sea

"There's a high tide tonight—the passenger with the bird mask in the gondola told us that," said Annie.

"Yeah, and winds from the south—the weather vane told us that," said Jack.

"And water's flowing down from the mountains—the woman at the café told us that," said Annie.

"Yeah, and storms out at sea—I saw lightning when we crossed the water," said Jack.

"All the conditions are here," said Annie.

Jack and Annie looked around. Water was now flowing steadily from the alleyways into the small square. It had risen above their ankles.

"I get it now," said Jack. "The water will just keep getting higher and higher until it destroys the whole city. And no one's paying attention!"

"Neptune's the only one who can help us stop the flood," said Annie.

"But Neptune's not real," said Jack. "I mean, he's a character in mythology, and mythology's not real life. It's—"

"Okay, okay," said Annie. "Let's just take one step at a time. At midnight two guys will tell us the time, and then we should climb to the top of their tower, right?"

"Right," said Jack.

"So what we have to do now is find those two guys!" said Annie.

"Let's go back to the waterfront," said Jack. "The man with the dog said everyone in Venice would be there for the fireworks."

Jack put away their book. Then he and Annie retraced their steps over the footbridge and back through the alleys. Lots of seaweed was floating in the narrow lanes between buildings. *Water is definitely flowing in from the sea,* Jack thought.

When they got back to Saint Mark's Square, people were streaming toward the waterfront. Jack and Annie walked with the crowd. Everyone was talking and laughing as they looked up at the sky over the water, waiting for the fireworks to begin. No one paid attention to the damp winds or the seawater spilling over the side of the canal, soaking their shoes.

"Excuse me!" Annie shouted. "Can anyone tell us the time?"

No one answered, for just then the first explosion of fireworks shook the night. The crowd cheered as blue and red showers exploded in the sky.

In the distance, a clock started to chime. Jack counted the bongs.

"Twelve!" he said. "It's midnight now, according to *that* clock."

More fireworks exploded over the waterfront, and another clock began clanging. This time, Jack counted only eleven bongs. He shook his head. "This is crazy!" he muttered.

Jack looked around at the crowd. "Can anyone tell us the real time?" he yelled. "Is it midnight yet? Can anyone tell us?"

No one answered—not even *one* man, much less two. Everyone was *oohing* and *aahing* over the dazzling fireworks.

Another clock began to sound. This one was much louder than the first two.

BONG!

"This is hopeless!" said Jack.

BONG!

"We'll never know the right time," he said.

BONG!

"Jack, look over there—" said Annie.

BONG!

"We'll never find the two men with the tower," said Jack.

BONG!

"Jack, look—" said Annie.

BONG!

"All of Venice is about to drown in a flood," said Jack.

BONG!

"And everyone's just cheering for fireworks!" said Jack.

BONG!

"JACK! LOOK!" said Annie. She pointed toward the clock tower in Saint Mark's Square.

BONG!

Jack saw a huge bell on top of the tower. Two bronze statues were holding a club and striking the bell.

BONG!

The statues were of *two men.*

BONG!

"At midnight two men will tell you the time," said Annie.

BONG!

The two men struck the bell for the twelfth time and then stopped.

"Come on!" cried Jack. "We have to climb that tower!"

More fireworks thundered over the canal as Jack and Annie pushed their way back through the crowd. They ran into Saint Mark's Square and splashed their way to the tall tower with the two men on top. They ran to the arched entrance of the tower and stepped inside. The air was damp and musty.

"Stairs!" said Jack. He ran to a dark, winding stairway and started up. Annie followed. They climbed and climbed until they reached the top of the tower.

Jack was breathing hard as he pushed open a heavy door that led out onto the bell terrace. The two statues were frozen on either side of the bronze bell.

As soon as Jack and Annie stepped onto the terrace, the wind blew their hats off their heads. The air was filled with cracking and hissing sounds as more fireworks burst through the sky. Everyone on the waterfront was clapping and cheering.

"What's the next thing Merlin tells us to do to find Neptune?" Annie shouted.

Jack pulled out Merlin's letter. Holding on to it tightly as it flapped in the wind, he read aloud:

The King of the Jungle will carry you there,
Not over land, but high in the air.

"The King of the Jungle is a lion," said Annie. "So it sounds like we need to find a flying lion!"

"Right," said Jack. "But where?"

"How about *that* one?" said Annie. She was pointing over the terrace railing.

Jack looked down. Standing on the wide ledge below was the stone statue of a lion. Growing out of the lion's back were two powerful-looking carved wings.

"But that's just a statue," cried Jack. "How can a statue take us anywhere?"

Annie grinned. "I think it's time to use a little more magic," she said.

CHAPTER SEVEN

The King and the Ruler

"Oh, yeah. Of course," whispered Jack. He'd forgotten all about Teddy and Kathleen's book of magic rhymes!

Jack pulled the book out of his backpack. He and Annie studied the table of contents. "*Make a Stone Come Alive,*" said Annie. "*Make Metal Soft. Turn into Ducks. Fly Through the Air—*that's it!"

"No," said Jack. "Go back to *Make a Stone Come Alive.*"

"Why?" said Annie.

"Because the lion's supposed to carry us," said Jack, "and he already has wings. But he's made of stone. So what we need to do is make him come alive."

"Oh, right," said Annie.

"But then what?" said Jack. "Where will we go?"

"Merlin's letter said an angel of gold would show us the way, remember?" said Annie.

"Angel of gold?" said Jack. "Where are we going to find that? And how will we find Neptune? How will he help us save Venice?"

"*Patience*," said Annie. "If we need more magic, we'll go back to the book."

"Okay. But let's hurry," said Jack. He opened Teddy and Kathleen's book to the second rhyme. He took a deep breath. He looked down at the lion on the ledge. Then he read in a loud, clear voice:

Stone so silent, cold, and hard,
Cum-matta-lie, cum-matta-skaard!

 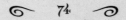

A cracking sound seemed to come from deep within the lion's body. As Jack and Annie peered down at the statue, the lion's stone mane ruffled into a mass of shaggy fur. His stone back softened into a sleek golden coat. His stone wings stretched into long, luminous feathers.

"Wow," breathed Annie. Jack couldn't speak. Before their eyes, the statue had turned into a living lion with magnificent golden wings. The lion shook his mane and yawned. He had huge, sharp teeth and a long pink tongue. His ears twitched. His tufted tail swayed back and forth.

The lion crouched and leapt off the ledge like a cat. He spread his wings and caught a strong current of wind. His wings flapped, and he began circling above the square.

"Here! Here!" Annie shouted. She waved wildly.

The winged lion turned and flew back toward the tower. He glided silently onto the terrace, landing just a few feet away from Jack and

Annie. He stared at them with his golden eyes.

"You have to help us save Venice from a flood disaster," Jack said.

"Can you carry us to Neptune?" said Annie.

The lion padded toward them. He kept staring straight at them. He tilted his tremendous head and let out a long growl, as if he was trying to answer.

"We have to climb on your back," said Jack.

"I hope we won't hurt you," said Annie.

The lion let out another growl, but he didn't sound angry. He sounded as if he was telling them to hurry. He crouched down so they could climb on.

"I'll go first," Jack said to Annie. "I'll hold on to his mane, and you hold on to me." Jack slipped off his backpack and dropped it onto the terrace.

"Take the book of rhymes," said Annie.

"Got it," said Jack. He tucked the book under his arm and carefully climbed onto the lion's back.

Annie climbed on behind Jack and wrapped her arms tightly around his waist. Jack twisted his fingers into the lion's mane. The mane felt surprisingly soft.

"Okay, we're ready," said Jack.

The lion stood up. He trembled slightly. Then he leapt off the terrace.

"Ahh!" Jack yelled. The rhyme book slipped from under his arm and fell down into the flooded square below.

"Oh, no! Our book!" cried Jack.

"Hang on!" cried Annie.

The lion flapped his great wings and rose through the sky. Jack pressed his knees into the lion's warm back and clung to his mane.

The lion flew toward the fireworks. A shower of red sparks was opening like an umbrella. Booms and whistles filled the night. Fiery bits rained down through the darkness, whistling into the canal.

"Help! We're heading straight into the fireworks!" cried Annie.

The lion dipped and turned away from the fireworks. The red showers gave way to bursts of blue and green.

"Which way do we go?" shouted Annie.

As the lion flew back toward the square, Jack saw the gold weather vane on top of the watchtower. *It was in the shape of an angel.*

"The angel of gold!" shouted Jack.

The weather vane was no longer pointing north with the winds. The angel was turning slowly around and around, pointing in all directions.

"Fly closer to the angel!" shouted Annie.

The lion turned and flew toward the watchtower. As they drew near the golden angel, Jack called out, "Which way do we go? Which way?"

The weather vane turned in a full circle and then came to a complete stop. The angel was pointing toward the southeast, over the choppy water.

"To the sea!" Annie called over the wind.

The lion turned and soared into the wind, his strong wings shining like gold.

"Oh, wow!" cried Annie.

The flying lion glided past the fireworks and over the wide canal. Leaving Venice behind, he flew high over the stormy seas.

Jack gripped the lion's mane with all his

might. The lion sailed in and out of thick, fast-moving clouds. He flew above crashing waves and past bolts of lightning. He flew through screaming winds and pelting rain.

In the middle of the sea, far from land, the lion began circling above the water. "What's he doing?" cried Jack.

"Looking for Neptune!" shouted Annie.

"But Neptune's not real!" said Jack.

"I know!" shouted Annie. "We'll have to use our imaginations! Like Lorenzo! Try to imagine Neptune!"

Jack tried to imagine Neptune, but he was too scared to think clearly.

"Neptune!" shouted Annie. "Rise from the water! Save Venice, Neptune! Help us!" Annie's voice was lost in the wind.

Jack wrapped his arms around the lion's neck. He buried his face in the lion's mane. He tried desperately to imagine Neptune.

The lion let out a roar. With his hands under

the lion's throat, Jack felt as if he himself were roaring. The lion roared again. The roaring made Jack feel stronger and calmer. The details of Tiepolo's painting came into his mind.

In his imagination, Jack saw Neptune, Ruler of the Seas, with his white beard and long hair, his strong arms and shoulders. He saw a lovely lady who was Venice, the Grand Lady of the Lagoon. . . . He saw Neptune giving the Grand Lady a gift. . . .

"I see something!" cried Annie.

Jack opened his eyes and sat up. "Where?" he cried.

"In the water!" said Annie.

Clinging to the lion's mane, Jack peered down into the darkness below. Lightning flashed over the sea. Jack saw a huge three-pronged spear rising out of the foaming, churning waves.

The sea below the spear began to heave and billow. Lightning flashed again, and Jack saw a great mass of swirling seaweed rising from the waves. *Not seaweed—hair!* Jack realized. A man's giant head and neck appeared above the surface of the water. Then the man's massive shoulders, chest, and arms rose above the storm-tossed sea. The giant loomed high above them, as tall as a mountain.

"Neptune!" cried Annie.

The lion let out a roar and then another and another.

Lit by flashes of lightning, Neptune's face looked as if it had been weathered by thousands of years of wind and sand and waves. He had deep-set eyes, craggy cheeks, a white beard, and tangled hair hanging to his shoulders.

"Neptune, save Venice from the flood!" cried Jack.

"Please!" called Annie. "Save the Grand Lady of the Lagoon!"

Neptune looked at them for a moment. Then, with his powerful arms, he lifted his spear and thrust it down into the waves. When the spear pierced the surface of the water, the sea made a gurgling sound—and then a long *slurp*, as if water were flowing down a drain.

The thunder and lightning stopped. The storm-tossed waves grew calm. The wind died to a gentle breeze. The clouds parted, and the stars shined brightly.

Neptune raised his spear. He nodded to Jack and Annie and the lion.

"Thanks!" cried Annie.

"Thanks!" shouted Jack. The lion roared again.

Then Neptune began to sink back into the sea. His long arms . . . huge shoulders . . . thick neck . . . craggy face . . . floating hair—all disappeared. The prongs of his spear sank below the surface of the water.

The Ruler of the Seas was gone. Only a shimmering whirlpool swirled in the moonlight.

CHAPTER EIGHT

Home by Day

Jack could hear the flapping of wings and the sound of steady breathing. The lion flew in circles above the whirlpool. Then he soared in a great arc up through the sky.

"We're going back now!" cried Annie.

Jack lowered his head. He buried his face again in the lion's shaggy, wet mane. He didn't look up. He was too tired to think as he gave himself over to the lion's wondrous powers of flight.

The lion carried Jack and Annie back through the dawn. As they glided over the calm sea, the waters sparkled with light from the rising sun.

By the time the lion reached the skies over Venice, darkness had turned to day. Shades of lavender glowed above the city's towers, domes, and spires. Venice was veiled in a soft pink light.

The lion flew to Saint Mark's Square. He glided toward the clock tower, moving more and more slowly. Finally, he landed softly, like a cat, on the terrace of the tower.

Jack took a deep breath and stroked the lion's golden mane. Then he and Annie climbed off the lion's back. Jack's legs felt wobbly. He clutched the lion for a moment to get his balance.

The lion let out a low growl. He turned his huge head and licked Jack's hand. His rough tongue felt like sandpaper. Jack laughed.

Annie laughed, too, as the lion licked her. "You were magnificent," she said.

"Yeah," said Jack. "That was a great ride."

The lion let out a long purr. Then he pulled away from the two of them and padded to the edge of the terrace.

The lion gave Jack and Annie one last look over his shoulder. Then he leapt over the terrace railing and landed silently on the ledge below.

Looking over the railing, Jack and Annie watched the living lion become a statue again. In an instant, his shaggy mane, golden back, powerful legs, tufted tail, and feathered wings all turned to carved gray stone.

"Oh," said Jack sadly. He missed the living lion hiding inside the stone statue.

A thundering *BONG!* made Jack and Annie

jump. Beside them, the two bronze men were striking their gigantic bell. They struck it six times.

"It's six in the morning," said Annie. "We were gone a long time."

"Yeah," said Jack.

"Hey, look at the angel weather vane now," said Annie.

Jack looked up at the gold angel on top of the watchtower. The weather vane was turning in the wind. It suddenly stopped and pointed toward the west.

"Remember the last lines from Merlin's letter?" said Annie. She recited them from memory:

An angel of gold will show you the way
To the sea by night, and home by day.

"I guess now that Venice is safe, the angel is telling us it's time to go home," said Jack.

"Yep," said Annie.

Jack picked up his backpack, and he and Annie headed down the stairs of the tower.

When they reached the bottom, they stepped out of the darkness into the bright morning light.

Only a few puddles of water dotted the square. Carnival had ended. The people in costumes had all gone home. A flock of pigeons fluttered noisily about the cobblestones, picking at orange peels, squashed grapes, torn ribbons, and feathers. There was no sign of the flood except for some patches of seaweed.

Jack turned and looked up at the clock tower. The morning sun cast a rosy light over the lion's stone body. The lion stood with pride and dignity, watching over Saint Mark's Square, his great powers a secret to everyone but Jack and Annie.

"Thanks again," said Annie to the lion.

"Yeah, thanks," whispered Jack. Then he sighed, exhausted. "Home?" he said. Annie nodded.

As Jack and Annie headed across the square, two sweepers were cleaning up the remains of Carnival.

"Oh, wow!" cried Annie. She ran toward the sweepers. Just as they were about to scoop up a pile of trash, she snatched something from the ground.

Annie ran back to Jack. "Look!" she said, and held up Teddy and Kathleen's book of magic rhymes.

"Oh, great!" said Jack. He took the little book from her. It was damp from the floodwaters, but all the writing was as clear as ever.

"We have eight rhymes left," said Jack, "for our next three journeys." He dropped the rhyme book into his backpack.

As Jack and Annie left Saint Mark's Square, they saw Venice starting to wake up—ordinary, everyday Venice, not the Venice of Carnival. Men, women, and children were opening stalls and putting out goods to sell. Cobblers were sitting at their workbenches, and cats were stretching in the chilly sunlight. The old man was walking his fat little dog, Rosa. He waved at Jack and Annie, and they waved back.

"No one knows Venice was almost destroyed by a flood last night," said Jack.

"And no one knows we helped save her," said Annie. "They just think we're a couple of ragged clowns."

Jack smiled. He'd forgotten they were still wearing their Carnival costumes. Now their clown suits were dirty, torn, and soaking wet. Their hats were gone. And somewhere, in the floodwaters or on the flight to Neptune, Jack's slippers had lost their bows.

"How will we get back to the tree house now?" asked Annie.

"I don't know," said Jack. "I guess we'll have to find a boat to take us there."

As they scanned the waterfront, Jack saw a boy sitting at the edge of the water on a small stool. The boy was painting.

"Hey, isn't that Lorenzo Tiepolo?" said Jack. He and Annie hurried over to the boy.

"Hi, Lorenzo!" said Annie.

Lorenzo glanced up and smiled. "Hello, Annie and Jack," he said.

Jack and Annie looked at Lorenzo's painting. It showed pink light shimmering on blue water. "That's beautiful," said Annie.

"It is only the background," said Lorenzo. He squinted at the canal. "Soon I will add gondolas and people. Then, probably, I will add something not real at all, something from my imagination."

"Hey, guess what! We saw Neptune last night," said Annie.

"You did?" said Lorenzo.

"We found him far out at sea," said Jack. "He looked just like he looks in your dad's painting."

"We rode to him on the back of the flying lion on the clock tower," said Annie.

Lorenzo nodded. "I am glad Neptune still lives in the deep sea," he said. "And I am glad one of our lions still flies. Many people believe all the magic has left our world."

"The magic will never leave," said Annie, "not if painters like you and your dad keep painting."

Lorenzo looked thoughtful. Then he picked up his small canvas and handed it to Jack. "You and Annie take this and finish it," he said. "Paint what you saw on your visit to Venice."

"Really?" said Jack. "Are you sure?"

"Yes," said Lorenzo. "You and Annie have the gift of imagination. Use it to make something magical."

"We will," said Annie.

"Thanks," said Jack. "We'll start painting as soon as we get home."

"Hey, Jack!" said Annie. She pointed at a gondola docked nearby. It looked like the same boat that had brought them to Carnival the night before. Inside were the same two people: the gondolier and the person with the lantern. Their

candle had gone out, but they were both still wearing black cloaks, white gloves, and masks with bird beaks.

"Maybe they can take us back to the tree house," said Jack.

"Excuse me," Annie called. "Can you give us a ride back to the island?" Annie pointed across the water.

The gondolier nodded.

"Great!" said Annie. "Bye, Lorenzo! Thanks!" And she and Jack hurried to the landing where the gondola waited for them.

CHAPTER NINE

The Painting

The gondolier silently helped Jack and Annie into the boat. Then he untied the gondola and pushed off from the landing.

As the boat glided through the shallow waters, Jack looked back at Venice. Bathed in early sunlight, the Grand Lady of the Lagoon *did* seem timeless.

The gondola moved around the bend and up the narrow canal near the walled garden. The gondolier tied the boat to a striped pole. He then offered his gloved hand to Annie to help her out of the boat. Annie climbed out and the gondolier offered his hand to Jack.

As the gondolier helped Jack onto the landing, the boat rocked in the water. Jack tripped, pulling the glove off the gondolier's hand.

"Oh, sorry," said Jack. As he handed the glove back, he gasped. *On the gondolier's finger was a pale blue glass ring.*

Before Jack could say anything, the gondolier pulled his glove back on and pushed the boat away from the landing.

"Hey—hey!" Jack sputtered. "Teddy? Kathleen? Wait! Come back!"

Neither of the masked people looked back at Jack and Annie.

"Teddy and Kathleen? Where?" said Annie.

"His glove—it came off! There was a blue glass ring on his finger!" said Jack.

Jack and Annie watched the gondola disappear into a blaze of sunlight shining on the water. Had it just glided around the bend? Or had it vanished altogether?

"Are you sure it was them?" said Annie.

"Well, I guess *anybody* could wear a glass ring," said Jack. "But still . . ."

"Maybe Morgan and Merlin told them to watch over us," said Annie.

"Yeah, to make sure we'd be safe," said Jack.

"And be patient and follow instructions," said Annie.

"Right," said Jack. "Well, Venice wasn't destroyed by a flood. So I guess we passed our first test."

"I think we did," said Annie.

With Lorenzo's canvas tucked under his arm, Jack led the way into the walled garden. Annie followed him to the rope ladder.

When they climbed into the tree house, Jack pulled Merlin's letter from his backpack. He unfolded it and pointed to the words *Frog Creek*.

"I wish we could go there!" he said.

"Good-bye, Grand Lady of the Lagoon!" said Annie.

The wind started to blow.

The tree house started to spin.

It spun faster and faster.

Then everything was still.

Absolutely still.

♦ ♦ ♦

A nippy wind rustled the Frog Creek trees. Jack and Annie were wearing their jeans and jackets again. It was dawn.

Annie sighed. "I wish we'd had a little more time to visit Venice," she said.

"I'm glad Lorenzo gave us his painting to finish," said Jack. "That'll be like living our trip all over again."

"Cool," said Annie.

"We'd better leave Morgan's research book here," said Jack. He pulled the book out of his backpack and put it on the floor. "And this." He took out Teddy and Kathleen's book of magic rhymes.

"Wait," said Annie. "Don't you think we should take the book of rhymes with us? For safekeeping?"

Jack nodded. "We can't use them in Frog Creek," he said. "We'll just keep it safe till we go on our next mission."

"That's what I was thinking," said Annie. "Come on. Hurry, before Mom and Dad wake up."

Jack put the book of rhymes back into his pack. Carrying Lorenzo's canvas, Annie climbed down the ladder. Jack followed.

As they walked through the chilly dawn woods, Annie held up Lorenzo's canvas. The shimmering light and waters of Venice looked just like they had in real life. "So what should we put in our painting?" she asked.

"Gondolas, of course," said Jack, "with people in costumes."

"Wearing black capes and bird masks," said Annie, "and fancy dresses and wigs."

"And we could paint the clock tower in the background," said Jack, "with the two men striking the bell."

"And the watchtower, too," said Annie, "with the gold angel on top."

"And the ruler's palace," said Jack.

"And the old man and Rosa walking along the canal," said Annie, "and, of course, Lorenzo."

"And the lion flying across the sky," said Jack, "and Neptune's spear rising out of the water."

"With Neptune himself peeking out!" said Annie. "We'll show just the top of his head and his mysterious eyes."

"That's a lot of stuff for one painting," said Jack.

"We didn't even put ourselves in yet," said Annie.

"We'll paint ourselves on the back of the lion," said Jack, "wearing our clown suits and red slippers."

"Yeah, with huge smiles on our faces," said Annie, "like we're thinking, *Wow! Wow! Wow!*"

Jack laughed.

A chilly dawn breeze swept through the bare trees. The bells of a Frog Creek church began to chime. Jack and Annie took off running for home.

More Facts About Venice

Venice has been called a "timeless city," as well as a city "frozen in time." This is because so much of the city and its traditions has been preserved through time.

The festival of Carnival goes back over a thousand years in Venice, but it was most popular during the 1700s.

Gondolas have glided along the waterways of Venice for over a thousand years. In the 1700s, there were about 14,000 on the canals. Today there are around 400.

Saint Mark the Apostle is the patron saint of Venice. According to legend, the saint's corpse was stolen from its grave and brought to Venice in the ninth century. Since the traditional symbol of Saint Mark is a winged lion, that image is depicted all over the city in paintings and sculptures. In Saint Mark's Square alone, there are no fewer than fourteen!

In Venice, there are approximately 3,000 alleys and 200 canals. Over 400 bridges connect 118 lagoon islands.

Many world-famous painters are from Venice. Giovanni Battista Tiepolo is considered the most important of the 1700s. His two sons, Giandomenico and Lorenzo, were also painters.

Neptune is the Roman counterpart of the sea god Poseidon from Greek mythology. Neptune's three-pronged fish spear is called a trident. When astronomers named the planet Neptune, they chose the trident to be its symbol.

Author's Research Note

Whenever I start work on a new Magic Tree House book, I begin the great adventure of research. I visit libraries, the Internet, bookstores, and museums. I talk to people who are knowledgeable about my subject, and if I'm able, I visit the place where the story occurs.

I chose to write a Magic Tree House story about Venice because I was eager to visit that wonderful city again. I had been to Venice a few years earlier, and when I returned home, I couldn't stop thinking about it. I especially remembered the warm summer night when I'd first stepped into Piazza San Marco, or St. Mark's Square. I remembered the beauty and magic of the square's architecture, the candlelit outdoor-café tables, and the sweet violin music played by musicians in tuxedos. I was dying to go back to Venice. What better excuse than to write a Magic Tree House book about the city and have a good reason to return?

On my second trip to Venice, I brought my guide book, camera, and notebook. I visited museums and bought books filled with paintings of Carnival costumes from the 1700s. I took photographs of the watchtower and the clock tower. I visited the Palazzo Ducale, or Doge's Palace, on the Piazza San Marco and took notes on the statues of Neptune and Mars, the paintings of the winged lions on the wall of the Map Room, and Giovanni Battista Tiepolo's painting *Neptune Offering Venice the Gifts of the Sea*, which now hangs in a palace chamber.

My most unforgettable experience in the Doge's Palace was a visit to the historic palace jail on the ground floor. I walked down a series of narrow, damp passageways and stone stairways and over the Bridge of Sighs until I came to the empty cells. In my notebook, I sketched diagrams of barred windows and heavy wooden doors.

As I tried to leave, I became confused about how to get out of the prison. Breathless, my heart pounding, I rushed through the musty-smelling passageways and up and down the steep stairways.

Finally I found my way back out onto the beautiful, sunny square. Once I had escaped from the palace, I happily thought, "Now, when I write about Jack and Annie's experience in the doge's jail, I'll *really* know how they would feel!"

On the morning I left Venice, I rode in a gondola and took notes on how the gondolier pushed his oar. I took notes on the pink early-morning light shimmering on the canal waters. I photographed the ancient city from offshore, trying to record its beauty and sense of timelessness. But no photographs can truly do Venice justice. No notes or diagrams can truly capture her. Venice lives best in memory, stirring the deep waters of the imagination.

Here's a special preview of

Magic Tree House #34
(A Merlin Mission)
Season of the Sandstorms

Jack and Annie go on another
amazing adventure filled with
history, magic, and lots of sand!

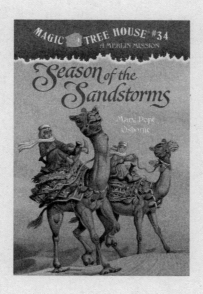

CHAPTER ONE

The Golden Age

Jack put his math homework aside. He opened the drawer beside his bed and pulled out a small, handmade book. For the hundredth time, he stared at the title on the cover:

10 MAGIC RHYMES FOR ANNIE AND JACK
FROM TEDDY AND KATHLEEN

For weeks, Jack had kept the book hidden in his drawer, wondering when he and Annie would be able to use its magic again. The book's ten rhymes were to be used on four missions, and each rhyme could be used only once. Jack and

Annie had already used two rhymes on a mission in Venice, Italy.

"Jack!" Annie rushed into Jack's room. Her eyes were shining. "Bring the book! Let's go!"

"Where?" said Jack.

"You know where! Come on!" Annie called as she ran back downstairs.

Jack quickly put Teddy and Kathleen's book into his backpack. He pulled on his jacket and took off down the stairs.

Annie was waiting on the front porch. "Hurry!" she cried.

"Wait! How do you know it's there?" Jack said.

"Because I just saw it!" Annie shouted. She hurried down the porch steps and crossed the yard.

"You saw it? Actually saw it?" yelled Jack as he followed Annie through the chilly afternoon air.

"Yes! Yes!" Annie yelled.

"When?" shouted Jack.

"Just now!" said Annie. "I was walking home from the library and I had this *feeling*—so I went and looked! It's waiting for us!"

Jack and Annie raced into the Frog Creek woods. They ran between the budding trees, over the fresh green moss of early spring, until they came to the tallest oak.

"See?" said Annie.

"Yes," breathed Jack. He stared up at the magic tree house. Its rope ladder dangled above the mossy ground. Annie started climbing up. Jack followed. When they got inside, Jack pulled off his backpack.

"Look, a book and a letter!" Annie said. She picked up a folded letter from the floor, and Jack picked up a book with a gold cover.

"Baghdad," Jack said. He showed the book to Annie. Its title was:

THE GOLDEN AGE OF BAGHDAD

"A golden age?" said Annie. "That sounds cool. Let's go!"

"Wait, we should read our letter first," said Jack.

"Right," said Annie. She unfolded the paper. "Merlin's handwriting," she said. She read aloud:

Dear Jack and Annie of Frog Creek,

Your mission is to journey to Baghdad of long ago and help the caliph spread wisdom to the world. To succeed, you must be humble and use your magic wisely. Follow these—

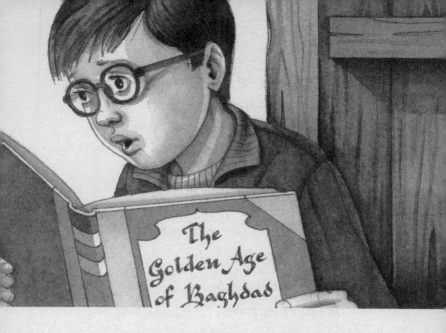

"Wait, what's a *caliph*?" said Jack. "And what's Merlin mean—'spread wisdom to the world'? That's a big responsibility."

"I don't know," said Annie. "Let me finish." She kept reading:

Follow these instructions:
Ride a ship of the desert
on a cold starry night.
Ride through the dust
and hot morning light.

Find a horse on a dome,
the one who sees all,
in the heart of the city
behind the third wall.

Beneath birds who sing
in the Room of the Tree,
greet a friend you once knew
and a new friend to be.

Remember that life
is full of surprises.
Return to the tree house
before the moon rises.

—M.

"This sounds pretty easy," said Annie.

"No, it doesn't," said Jack. "All these instructions are so mysterious. We don't know what any of them mean."

"We'll find out when we get there," said Annie. "But first we have to get there. Make the wish."

"Okay," said Jack. He pointed to the cover of

the book. "I wish we could go to the golden age of Baghdad," he said.

The wind started to blow.

The tree house started to spin.

It spun faster and faster.

Then everything was still.

Absolutely still.

Discover the facts
behind the fiction with the

MAGIC TREE HOUSE®
RESEARCH GUIDES

The must-have, all-true companions for your
favorite Magic Tree House® adventures!

Guess what?
Jack and Annie are onstage!

For more information on
MAGIC TREE HOUSE: THE MUSICAL
(including how to order the CD!), visit
www.mthmusical.com.

About the Illustrator

Sal Murdocca is best known for his amazing work on the *Magic Tree House* series. He has written and/or illustrated over two hundred children's books, including *Dancing Granny* by Elizabeth Winthrop, *Double Trouble in Walla Walla* by Andrew Clements, and *Big Numbers* by Edward Packard. He has taught writing and illustration at the Parsons School of Design in New York. He is the librettist for a children's opera and has recently completed his second short film. Sal Murdocca is an avid runner, hiker, and bicyclist. He has often bicycle-toured in Europe and has had many one-man shows of his paintings from these trips. He lives and works with his wife, Nancy, in New City, New York.